Rubber Duck

Written by Dana Meachen Rau
Illustrated by Patrick Girouard

Reading Advisers:

Gail Saunders-Smith, Ph.D., Reading Specialist

Dr. Linda D. Labbo, Department of Reading Education,
College of Education, The University of Georgia

LEVEL C

A COMPASS POINT
EARLY READER

For Pavinee, Tim, and the boys

A Note to Parents

As you share this book with your child, you are showing your new reader what reading looks like and sounds like. You can read to your child anywhere—in a special area in your home, at the library, on the bus, or in the car. Your child will associate reading with the pleasure of being with you.

This book will introduce your young reader to many of the basic concepts, skills, and vocabulary necessary for successful reading. Talk through the details in each picture before you read. Then read the book to your child. As you read, point to each word, stopping to talk about what the words mean and the pictures show. Your child will begin to link the sounds of the letters with the look of the words that you and he or she read.

After your child is familiar with the story, let him or her read the story alone. Be careful to let the young reader make mistakes and correct them on his or her own. Be sure to praise the young reader's abilities. And, above all, have fun.

Gail Saunders-Smith, Ph.D.
Reading Specialist

Compass Point Books
3722 West 50th Street, #115
Minneapolis, MN 55410

Visit Compass Point Books on the Internet at *www.compasspointbooks.com* or e-mail your request to *custserv@compasspointbooks.com*

Library of Congress Cataloging-in-Publication Data
Rau, Dana Meachen, 1971–
    Rubber duck / written by Dana Meachen Rau ; illustrated by Patrick Girouard.
      p. cm. — (Compass Point early reader)
    Summary: A rubber duck leaves his clean bathtub and has messy adventures outside.
    ISBN 0-7565-0121-0 (hardcover : library binding)
    [1. Toys—Fiction. 2. Stories in rhyme.] I. Girouard, Patrick, ill. II. Title. III. Series.
PZ8.3.R232 Ru 2001
[E]—dc21   2001001598

You look bored, rubber duck.
You sit inside all day.

Forget the tub. Come with me.

Let's go outside to play!

4

See my new, red, shiny bike?
I'll take you on a ride.

I'll catch you at the bottom
when you tumble down the slide.

MAX

Now let's give this bug a lift.
He'll sit right on your tail.

Let's hide from my big sister
behind this garbage pail.

Now let's rake together leaves
and jump into the pile.

You like it when I bury you.
I know it by your smile.

Roll down this grassy, muddy hill.
I'll let you win first place.

Rubber duck, it's hard to tell
if that is really you.

Your yellow body and orange beak are covered up with goo!

Let's go inside.

I'll run the water

and give your back a scrub.

Did you like to play outside
or do you like the tub?

Everyone loves playing with toys. Some toys are inside toys and some toys belong outside. Try the following activity with your child. Point to each of the toys pictured below. Which toys belong inside? Which ones belong outside?

Encourage your child's creativity on the next rainy or sunny day—if it is a nice day, ask your child to think of things they can do outside that they usually do inside, such as read a book under a tree or take a walk with a teddy bear. On a rainy day, ask your child to think of things they can do inside that they usually do outside, such as have a picnic on the kitchen floor or play hide and seek in the bedroom.

Word List

(In this book: 105 words)

a	hard	really
all	he'll	red
and	hide	ride
are	hill	right
at	I	roll
back	I'll	rubber
beak	if	run
behind	inside	scrub
big	into	see
bike	is	shiny
body	it	sister
bored	it's	sit
bottom	jump	slide
bug	know	smile
bury	leaves	stick
by	let	tail
catch	let's	take
come	lift	tell
covered	like	that
day	look	the
did	marshmallows	these
do	me	they
down	muddy	this
duck	my	to
eat	new	together
face	now	tub
first	on	tumble
forget	or	up
from	orange	water
garbage	outside	when
give	pail	win
gluey	pile	with
go	place	yellow
goo	play	you
grassy	rake	your

About the Author

Dana Meachen Rau loves to play with her son Charlie—digging in the outdoor sandbox, drawing with chalk on the driveway, and chasing him in his scooter. And they always get very dirty. But part of the fun is cleaning up when they get inside. Dana takes a shower, and Charlie takes a bath, but Dana does not let Charlie take his rubber duck outside. When Dana isn't playing or cleaning up, she's writing books in her office in Farmington, Connecticut.

About the Illustrator

Patrick Girouard has been drawing and painting for many years. He lives in Indiana.